The Adventures of
Phil & Lill

by Ernest Henry
Pictures by Keith Smith

Hill's

Hill's Pet Nutrition

Bloomsbury Children's Books

CHAPTER 1
The Kittens Find a Home

The little kittens peeped timidly through a tiny opening made by the worn blanket draped over the old cat basket held by the Man From The Cat Home.

A big black door loomed up in front of them out of the cold, misty night, getting bigger as they climbed up the long steps.

"Oh, dear," murmured the boy kitten, nervously.

"Don't worry. It'll be all right – this time. And I'm here," said his sister reassuringly. The two kittens had been abandoned at birth and had spent all their short lives in a cat home until somewhere permanent could be found for them to live. There were too many cats at the home for them to have had much attention – and a cuddle or two. But at least they had been safe, and dry, and out of the cold.

Suddenly the big black door opened, and a little Boy with fizzing hair, bright, clever eyes and a huge grin, appeared in a shaft of golden light shining out into the dark night.

He looked excitedly at the basket. "They're here! They're here!" he shouted, and immediately a Girl, bigger than the Boy, and a Lady came rushing to see.

"Hallo, hallo!" the Lady welcomed. "Come in out of the cold," and the Man From The Cat Home wiped his feet on the doormat, entered the warm hallway, he and the kittens leaving the dark, damp, icy December night behind.

They followed the Lady along the hallway into a big room.

"Let me see, let me see," said the little Boy, beside himself with joy, and the Man lifted the blanket and two pairs of little eyes blinked up through the grating of the old basket.

"Hallo," the Boy squealed, bending over to take a closer look. "Can I hold them, can I?" Very gently the Man opened the top of the basket and lifted the two little kittens out of the box and put them on the wooden floor of the sitting room.

The boy kitten – a browny-grey tabby, slightly smaller than kittens his age – looked around, and then up at the Boy. He then rolled over on his back, like a dog. His sister – a beautiful and delicate English Tortic with eyes big as saucers and a cream and brown strip in the middle of her chin – looked on... and then she, too, looked up at the Boy, both pleading with the family to be taken in.

They needn't have worried, though. The little Boy – his name was Hugo – and his elder sister, Claire and their Mum all agreed, there was NO WAY these little kittens were going ANYWHERE!!

Hugo picked up the little boy kitten and held him close, and Claire did the same with the sister.

"We're going to call you Phil and Lill," Hugo said in his usual definitive way.

Phil looked across at Lill, each in one of the children's arms, a tear in his eye. "I-I-I think we've found a home, Lill," he said.

"Yes, I think we have," replied Lill, snuggling up into Claire's arms.

CHAPTER 2
Safe at Last

When the Man From The Cat Home had finally gone, Phil and Lill were placed on a blanket in the middle of one of the white sofas in the sitting room.

"I-I-I think I'll like it here," said Phil, with a wheeze and a cough.

"I *know I* do," replied Lill.

Just then, though, the Lady – "her name's MUM, Lill," informed Phil – picked up Phil and took him up some stairs to a Strange Room with three tub-like things in it – one of which was filled with water!

"Here, 'ere, 'ere. What's going on?" asked Phil,

starting to struggle a little bit.

As if understanding what he was saying, Hugo replied, "Don't worry, Phil. You're just going to have a little wash, as you're a bit grubby, you know." And with that Phil, and then afterwards Lill, were washed ever so gently with very special cat shampoo by Mum.

Water and some good food had been prepared in two new bowls, and Phil and Lill were placed carefully in front of them, so they should know that it was eating time.

Phil didn't need any telling. "Oh – foody bits, Lill," he said, cautiously sniffing inside the bowl before tucking in.

"They smell really good, too," replied Lill, and she started to munch away.

Phil didn't eat much. It was very clear by the way he moved, wheezed and coughed that he wasn't a well pussy cat.

"Mum says we're going to the vet tomorrow morning," Lill told Phil later, after they were tucked up snoogy warm in a blue and white check baby blanket.

"Oh!" replied Phil. "What's a vet?"

CHAPTER 3
A Visit to the Vet

"Hallo! Who have we here?" The Vet beamed at Phil as he lifted him gently from the box and placed him onto the examining table.

"My name's Phil," replied Phil, rolling over on his back again making everyone laugh!

The Vet made a thorough examination first of Phil, then Lill, chatting gently to them all the time. He gave Phil some medicine and an injection to treat his cold and told Mum all about their condition, what they should have to make them well and general stuff about caring for kittens.

"What's he doing now?" asked Phil.

"I think he's giving Mum 'structions," replied Lill.

"What's 'structions?" asked Phil.

"'Structions is telling someone what to do," replied Lill wisely.

"Oh," said Phil – still not understanding properly.

The Vet was very happy that Phil and Lill were already eating food at home which would keep them well and which he used in his surgery. So all in all it was a good visit and the kittens were soon back at home.

"It's nice to be in Cozy Warm again, isn't it, Phil," said Lill.

But Phil had curled up on their blanket and had dozed off. It had been a tiring and busy morning for such a little chap.

CHAPTER 4
Discovering What's What!

For a short while, the kittens were kept in one room, so that they'd start to feel secure.

But very soon ALL the doors were opened and Phil and Lill were able to explore their new home.

The better they got to know the place, the faster they'd dash about.

Phil liked jumping around. "I-I-I'm a tiger," he'd say as he bounced around on all the furniture.

Until, that is, he crashed into a favourite vase.

"Naughty boy!!" shouted Claire, which made Phil extremely piffy: "Not only have I not been very well, but I've been shouted at, too." And he'd go off in a huff!

Phil and Lill liked to settle down on the back of the sofa in the television room after their mid-morning foody bits. They'd sigh at each other, the fading memory of the old cat home and darker days getting dimmer as time wore happily on.

It would be at quiet moments like this that Lill would think up little rhymes and ditties:

I'd rather be here in the Inside World
Looking out to the Outside World:
It's cozy warm in the Inside World,
Safe and snuggly and curled.

It's all very strange in the Outside World:
Busy and whizzy and cold.
So I think I'll stay here in the Inside World
And grow lazy and happy and old.

CHAPTER 5
The Great Surprise

...And very soon it was early spring, and the Outside World became warmer.

So they could go and explore, Phil and Lill had their injections and were each given collars which Hugo and Claire ceremoniously placed around their necks.

"Look, Phil," said Lill. "I've got my brand new collar."

Isn't it beautiful
It's got a silver bell
And a dingle dangle
In which it can tell
Anyone who looks inside
Its pretty silver form
That my name is Lill
And I live at Cozy Warm.

"I got a collar, too," said Phil, indignantly. "I can go outside now and get into mischief and things and stay out in the rain and run about like a tiger!"

"There's no foody bits and cozy warm outside, Phil," warned Lill as she put her little head around the Big Front Door for the first time and sniffed, eyes as big as saucers.

"Oh – I-I-I'll always be back in time for foody bits... and won't go far, anyway," said Phil, joining her, gazing out in wonder. "Cor!"

The house only had one door to the outside – the Big Front Door.

Lill decided that the best point of entry or exit would be the windows in the tv room. It was an easy hop from the porch at the top of the front doorsteps to the ledge running outside the windows. So long as they were open, Lill discovered she could come in or go out at leisure.

Phil disagreed. He decided the proper way in or out was through the door – so much more dignified – and tiger-like!

He'd meow in the hall – "I-I-I'd like to go out now, please." And he'd meow – loudly – on the front porch when he wanted to come in again.

CHAPTER 6
Phil has an Adventure

Each evening, Mum would go to the Big Door and call the kittens in: "Leeeeeeeeyal! Pheeeeeeeeyal! Coooooome!" And Phil and Lill would come scuttling into the house: Lill, through the window, Phil, through 'his' door.

One particular evening, Mum and Claire went to the Big Door. "Leeeyal! Pheeeyal! Coooooome!" went out the call. Sure enough, in came Lill.

"Here I am," she meowed sharply, announcing her arrival and dashing straight for the bowls. "I'm home. I've had such a busy afternoon with all my friends."

Mum and Claire stayed by the door for another five minutes waiting for Phil.

"Pheeeyal! Pheeeeeelie! Cooooome!" But Phil didn't come.

"Oh, dear," said Claire. "I hope he's all right. He's still very little."

"I should think he'll come back soon," said Mum. "Cats do go off sometimes, you know. Anyway, people will know he has a home and isn't a stray because he has his collar on."

"Oh, no, he hasn't," chimed Hugo joining them at the door, holding Phil's collar, which had somehow come off.

"Well, he'd better come home soon," said Claire, "'cause it's starting to rain."

"Cor," said Phil. "This is a real 'venture." He'd discovered a building site a few streets away from his own house and was having great fun playing pretending games: 'No Emenies'. Phil peeped out from under a tent-like awning covering bags of cement and sand. There weren't any 'emenies' so he scuttled around planks of wood, and over piles of building stuff, getting quite excited by the fun of it all.

He noticed a fresh wind and a few drops of rain on his little nose and leapt into a hidey-hole under some piles of wood leaning against a wall at the front of the house.

But as the rain started to pelt down really hard,

and with it the wind, little Phil's hiding place was fast becoming anything but safe, or dry.

"I-I-I'd better get out of here." A little tremor crept into his voice.

He walked out into the stormy rain, looking first left and then right trying to decide which route would take him home.

His fur was soaking, and drops of rain dripped from his long eye lashes.

"I-I-I don't know which way to go." A lump welled up in his throat. "Where's Cozy Warm?"

He tried to be brave. But it was cold and he was hungry.

"I-I-I don't like this." He jumped into a skip full of rubbish and stuff, and sheltered under an old door. At least it would be dry there, he thought.

"I wish I was in Cozy Warm with Lill, and could have some foody bits and water" – his tummy rumbled – "and a cuddle from Hugo."

Phil closed his eyes and fell asleep.

Lill curled up alone at home on the soft blue and white chequered blanket. "I hope Phil's all right," she sighed. "I do hope he's all right." Tears filled her lovely eyes big as saucers, and she drifted off into an unhappy sleep.

CHAPTER 7
Phil Goes for a Ride

Claire and Hugo burst into their Mum and Dad's bedroom early next morning.

"Phil's still not here. He's disappeared!" they cried.

Immediately a plan of action was drawn up by Dad: Operation Find Phil. Lost cat notices – lots of them – were prepared by Hugo on vivid yellow card paper to be pinned up all over the neighbourhood.

Claire, Hugo and Dad then raced around, calling at people's houses to

enquire whether anyone had seen their Phil.

No one had.

Phil woke early that morning too. He stretched his legs and body as he usually did, but felt a bit strange."

"Oh! I-I-I'm stuck!" Something was pinning him down and no matter how hard he tried, he couldn't struggle free.

"I must be calm. Now: what would a tiger do?"

His only answer was the clanging noise of chains. Machinery. Men shouting instructions to one another. An engine roaring away.

"Oouu-er," said Phil. "What's happening?"

The skip was being collected by a truck to be

driven off on to a rubbish dump somewhere. But the jolt of lifting must have moved the object pinning Phil in place, and he was able to wriggle free at last.

He dashed up the rubbish and was about to jump off the skip and into the street when he screeched to a stop at the edge. He discovered he was a long, long way off the ground.

"Meooowww!" he called.

"Hey – someone! Look! I'm here! Can you let me off?"

But the truck shunted off down the road at high speed.

Luckily, there was a junction at the bottom of the road, so the truck had to stop. Phil seized his opportunity to leap off the back of the skip, just as the contraption began to pull away again.

"That was a near thing."

Catching his breath on the pavement, Phil looked about him and started wandering up the road, tired, hungry – and lost.

It was when he was making one of his

occasional stops to see if he could recognise anything, that he heard a kindly voice. He looked up and saw a lady smiling down at him.

"What have we here? Are you lost, then? You look jolly hungry, too," the Kindly Voice said. "Have you a collar? Let me see – no. Oh, dear, another poor stray," the Voice sighed.

And because he was tired and hungry, Phil was off his guard for a moment, and the kind lady was able to grab him by the scruff of his neck and bundle him in her arms.

"Oh, you're very sweet."

She looked down at Phil and took him to her flat for some food and milk.

"Ah, foody bits." Phil leapt at the bowl, sniffed, but wasn't too sure whether he liked what he smelled.

"S'not the same as I get at Cozy Warm," he grumbled.

Food over, Phil trotted into the lady's sitting room, where she was talking on the phone.

It was a gloomy flat, thought Phil. The windows all had net curtains on them and a ledge full of fussy plant pots.

"What are you doing?" the lady said kindly, taking him down just as he'd leapt up to have a look out.

In that very moment, however, Phil saw something he knew – something he knew very well.

"Cozy Warm! Cozy Warm!" he yelped, his head craning to see out of the window again as he struggled to get out of the lady's grip.

"It is! It is!" he meowed to the lady excitedly. "Why can't she understand? Mum understands everything I say. Why can't this lady?"

But the lady only held him more firmly and said, "Naughty boy. I'll have to put you in the spare room and close the door, otherwise you'll knock over all my precious plants, and that won't do at all. No, it won't."

And she carried him into the other room.

"Now you stay here and in the morning the nice man from the cat home will come and pick you up and take you to a lovely place, full of other cats to play with."

She closed the door.

Phil froze.

"The Man From The Cat Home," he trembled, his distant cat memory conjuring up vivid pictures of dark times, long ago.

"I-I-I can't go back. I can't go back," he started to cry and wandered around the miserable little room. He looked up and through his tears saw another window. He jumped up onto its ledge and peered out.

"Cozy Warm," he blurted. "Oh, Cozy Warm," he sobbed, gazing out of the window, longingly.

Night came, and Phil could make out the figures of Claire and Hugo, Mum and Dad through the windows of the house he knew so well and loved so much. He couldn't see Lill, but he imagined her, and let out a heart-broken cry.

At that moment, just across the road, so near yet so far, Lill lifted her head suddenly, as if she'd heard something.

"What's the matter, Lill?" asked Claire.

"Ooooow," came the mournful reply.

CHAPTER 8
The Great Escape

The knock came at 8.30 on the dot. Phil heard voices in the hall outside the little room in which he'd spent a long and lonely night.

The voices came nearer. The door opened, slowly... and there, standing in front of him, was The Man From The Cat Home.

Phil's nostrils twitched. He recognised the smell and backed away from the man, who was bending down now, offering cat treats in one hand, whilst holding a wire cage in the other.

"Good boy," the man said, not, however, recognising Phil. "Come along. I've got lots of friends for you to play with."

But Phil had trapped himself in a corner. The man lunged, grabbed and dropped him straight into the cage, locking the lid shut all in one abrupt movement.

The man said goodbye and thanks to the lady and went to leave.

"Just a minute," she said. "I nearly forgot. Let the poor little thing have these," and the lady opened the lid of the cat cage and dropped some special treats inside for the journey.

As she did so, Phil took his chance. Summoning up all the courage and strength of the tiger he *really*

was, he leapt out of the cage and bounded out of
the lady's flat, downstairs and into the street.

Once outside, Phil turned and gave
a triumphant, thundering roar,
(which actually came out a
loud meow), announcing
gravely that he *was* a tiger
and dashed off across the
road to Cozy Warm.

CHAPTER 9
Home Again

"Meow," Phil roared, standing on the porch on the outside of the Big Door.

Everyone on the inside heard it, and there was a frantic dash down the long hallway to the Big Door, which was opened in a matter of seconds.

And there was Phil!

"I-I-I'm back," he looked up into the faces looking

lovingly down at him. Lill came bounding over.

"Where have you been, Phil?" she scolded. "We've been worried sick."

"I-I-I-I was having a 'venture," replied Phil, but Hugo scooped the kitten up in his arms.

"I-I-I was being a tiger," continued Phil, choking back a sob, and straining to look down at Lill while perched in Hugo's arms way above her head.

"Oh, Phil," replied Lill, cross but so happy to see him again.

"It went a bit wrong, Lill... I don't think I'm going for another 'venture — not for a while, at least."

Phil had his foody bits and water, and afterwards he jumped up on the sofa and snuggled down on his soft blue and white chequered blanket. Claire and Hugo, Mum, Dad and Lill all looked at him, safe home again.

"From now on, Phil," Mum said, wagging her finger in a smiley strict sort of way, "you come back in half an hour, now. Half an hour!"

"That's no way to treat a tiger," said Phil, but he beamed up at them and went peacefully to sleep.

40